MARK ROBERTSON studied Graphic Design at Kingston University.
A freelance illustrator since 1988, he specialises in children's books.
His previous books for Frances Lincoln are *Seven Ways to Catch the Moon*,
The Egg, *Ice Trap!* by Meredith Hooper, *The Sandcastle*,
Edison's Fantastic Phonograph by Diana Kimpton and
Seven Wonders of the Ancient World by Mary Hoffman.
Mark lives with his family in Wiltshire.

For Holly and Tess –
the giggliest twins in the world

Big Foot copyright © Frances Lincoln Limited 2002
Text and illustrations copyright © M.P. Robertson 2002

First published in Great Britain in 2002 by
Frances Lincoln Limited, 4 Torriano Mews,
Torriano Avenue, London NW5 2RZ

www.franceslincoln.com

First paperback edition 2003

British Library Cataloguing in Publication Data
available on request

ISBN 0-7112-2068-9 paperback
ISBN 0-7112-1945-1 hardback

Set in Clearface

Printed in Singapore
9 8 7 6 5 4 3

BiG FooT

M.P. Robertson

FRANCES LINCOLN

There's a creature lurking in the deep dark woods. At night he sings his sad song to an ice cold moon.

One fat moon night I heard his song.
I opened my window and played a tune
to the trees. There came a sad reply.
   He was very lonely. He needed a friend!

I climbed out into the crisp cold. He had left a trail
of footprints. He had very big feet – even bigger
than my dad's. I will call him 'Big Foot', I decided.

I followed his trail as it wove deeper
and deeper into the dark woods.

Snow began to fall silently. It laid a white blanket
over the trail. I would never find Big Foot now.

I turned towards home, but each tree looked
the same as the last.

The forest had swallowed me up.

I sat down and shivered beneath the ice cold moon.

I took out my flute and played a warming tune.

Then suddenly something stirred. Something BIG… something HAIRY! As tall as a tree but with gentleness in his eyes.

It was Big Foot.

"I'm lost," I sobbed. "Can you show me the way home?"

He brushed an icicle tear from my cheek, then lifted me on to his broad shoulders, and together we bounded through the trees.

At the edge of the forest we came to a slope.

It was too steep to walk down.

Big Foot lay down and I rode him
like a hairy sledge.

At the bottom was a frozen lake. It was too slippery
to walk across, so we used icicles as skates.

Big Foot was very graceful for one so hairy.

When we reached the other side of the lake,
I challenged Big Foot to a snowball fight.

I think he won!

"We should build a snowman," I said.

Big Foot scraped up a mountain of snow and began to sculpt. But he didn't make a snowman – he made a snow Big Foot.

When it was finished, Big Foot looked at it sadly, as though he wished it were real. He wanted another Big Foot – someone to be his friend.

I brushed an icicle tear from his cheek and kissed his hairy face. "I know I'm not a Big Foot," I said, "but I will be your friend."

I suddenly felt very tired. Big Foot rested me on his back.
As we lolloped through the trees I drifted into warm sleep.

In the morning, Big Foot had gone.

That evening I played my flute to the trees,
but there was no reply.

Every evening I did the same, but Big Foot
never answered. Had he been just a winter dream?

Then one fat moon night as I played a tune
to the trees, I heard his song at last. He no longer
sounded sad, and as I played, his song was joined
by another.

Big Foot had found a friend.

MORE TITLES BY MARK ROBERTSON IN PAPERBACK FROM FRANCES LINCOLN

THE EGG

When George discovers a rather large egg under his mother's favourite chicken, he soon finds himself looking after a baby dragon. But the dragon begins pining for its own kind, and one day it disappears …

Suitable for National Curriculum English – Reading, Key Stages 1 and 2
Scottish Guidelines English Language – Reading, Levels A, B and C

ISBN 0-7112-1525-1

SEVEN WAYS TO CATCH THE MOON

There are seven ways to catch the moon … Follow a young girl's dream as she tries hitching with a witch, riding on a dragon's back and floating in a hot-air balloon, in this beautifully illustrated fantasy.

Suitable for National Curriculum English – Reading, Key Stage 1
Scottish Guidelines English Language – Reading, Level A

ISBN 0-7112-1413-1

THE SANDCASTLE

Jack loves building sandcastles more than anything in the world. But he can't stop the sea from stealing them away. One day he finds a shell with magical powers, but is his new power greater than the power of the sea?

Suitable for National Curriculum English – Reading, Key Stage 1
Scottish Guidelines English Language – Reading, Levels A and B

ISBN 0-7112-1807-2

Frances Lincoln titles are available from all good bookshops.
You can also buy books and find out more about your favourite titles, authors and illustrators at our website:
www.franceslincoln.com.